BÊTE NOIRE

FEAR IS JUST A POINT OF VIEW

Editors:

A. W. Gifford

Jennifer L. Gifford

www.betenoiremagazine.com

Bête Noire is published by Dark Opus Press a division of Charm Noir Omnimedia

ISBN-13: 987-0692588642
ISBN-10: 0692588647

"The Patron Saint of Rubberneckers" by Noel Sloboda, first appeared in *Falling Star*

"They always Come in Twos" by Adam Gaylord, first appeared in *Plasma Frequency Magazine*, November 2013

In This Issue

THE BIG BLUFF

Dusty Wallace

A sudden turbulence broke the water's calm surface. Virgil and I started pulling in the tether immediately. It was still knotted around Mick's waist when his headless corpse surfaced. He must have been fiddling with the lock as the briefcase rested on the lake bottom. The booby trap had left everything from the neck down in mint condition. Tattered rags of wet-suit hung limply from the stump of his neck.

"Shark," Virgil said.

"Dude, it's a fucking fresh-water lake," I told him.

"Exactly." Virgil nodded knowingly.

"Virgil are you really that fucking stupid? We're on a lake in the Appalachian Mountains of Virginia. There are no fucking sharks here." He stared at me dumbly. "It was a fucking trap, you idiot!"

"Why you gotta be so mean, Johnny?"

I ignored the question and untied the anchor from the rail of our rented pontoon. Leaning over the edge, I replaced Mick's guide-rope with the anchor's line and tossed the hunk of metal into the water. When the rope reached its limit Mick's body jolted a bit then disappeared into the lightless depths, a trail of blood dissipating as he sunk.

Back at the dock, I had Virgil tie us off while I entered the cabin to have a chat with Fat Sal.

Sal was a capo from a Chicago family. He was in Franklin County on a moonshine run. That old white lightnin' was a favorite of the Italian-Chicagoan community dating back to prohibition. I had figured out Sal's schedule after a few months of surveillance. Virgil and I tossed a burlap potato sack over his head when he stopped for a piss in the woods along the Booker T. Washington Highway. In the end, Fat Sal was captured thanks to a small bladder and large prostate.

"Back so soon?" Sal quipped as I entered the one-room log cabin.

Also a rental.

"I think you owe me an explanation," I said.

Fat Sal said, "I always figured some redneck *jamook* would have at me one of these days. Planted that briefcase years ago. Did it work?" I didn't know what *jamook* meant, but I resented being called a redneck. I'd read the classics, after all. Besides, hillbilly was a more accurate term, what with the mullet, cutoff jeans, and stained wife-beater. Virgil was black, but still more a redneck than myself. He was the one wearing overalls with for Christ's sake.

"We'd have to ask Mick, unfortunately he's lying headless at the bottom of the lake," I said.

"Cleaner place to rest than the Chicago river, at least," Sal said with a grin.

"I doubt very much that Mick gives a shit. Then again, Mick is a dickhead and I'd rather have killed him than cut him in on the deal anyway," I said.

"Silver linings," Sal said.

"Now how 'bout you tell me where the fuck you hid the money? We tore up that damn Cadillac of yours. Didn't find it in the trunk, floorboard, or hidden under the chassis."

"Did you try the glove department?" Sal asked sardonically.

I introduced Sal's jaw to the back of my fist. My hand stung like a bitch but it didn't seem to faze him.

Sal said, "Do you jerk off with the other hand? Maybe you'll hit harder with that one."

I'm not exactly a pro, and Virgil's too stupid to be anything but a cronie, so we didn't have any instruments of torture lying around. Until being laid off a year ago, we'd been upholstery men at a furniture factory in Bassett. Since then we'd been sharing an efficiency apartment and living on unemployment. Career criminals we were not.

Virgil joined us in the cabin. "Motherfucker tell you where the cheddar at?"

"Not yet," I said.

Sal said, "Not ever."

"I'll tell you what," I said. "You tell us where you stashed the money and we'll split it with you and let you go unharmed."

Fat Sal laughed boisterously. "Fucking amateurs." I couldn't deny that one.

"Fuck you, you fat fucking piece of fuck," Virgil yelled and marched towards Sal.

I stepped in his way, putting my hand on his shoulders. "Chill out, man. Go have a seat and relax. I got this."

Thirty minutes and three joints later, Virgil was laying on the couch and staring into some fractal vortex of color invisible to all but himself. A dumb smile curled his lips revealing missing teeth, a jack-o-lantern smile.

I polished off two or three cocktails. Lemondrops, if you must know, with a little umbrella in the glass. Suddenly a plan started to manifest from the ethanol. I needed to get supplies, though.

"Virgil, keep an eye on Fat Sal." Virgil stared off into his own private wormhole. I'd be lucky if he didn't cut Sal free on the promise of cookies while I was gone. "Try not to piss yourself," I said to him.

"After visiting Wal-Mart and Radioshack I came back to the cabin. First, I brought in a spool of copper wire, leaving one end at Virgil's feet and unspooling backwards through the door.

Outside, with the door open for Fat Sal's viewing pleasure, I affixed the wire to a small, battery-powered switch.

I carried in an object wrapped in brown paper. Kneeling in front of Sal's bound legs, I carefully unfolded the paper revealing a squared chunk of plastic explosives.

After attaching the wires, I stuffed the C-4 down the front of Fat Sal's oversized Armani pants. Like a dog humping its owner's leg, he thrust his crotch in a vain effort to rid himself of the explosives.

I turned to Virgil, now sleeping on the couch. "It's time to go."

He snorted but didn't open his eyes.

I slapped him lightly on the cheek. "Time to get the fuck out of Dodge," I said.

"What's up? He tell you where the money's at?" Virgil asked.

"Nope, he's gonna take that one to the grave," I said.

"Aight. Fuck it." Virgil stood and made for the door.

Fat Sal still tried to look tough but was betrayed by the sweat pouring from his brow. "You don't wanna do this," he said.

"You're right. But you've left me no choice," I said.

"That's right, motherfucker. We gon' feed yo' ass to the sharks," Virgil said.

Sal gave me a puzzled look. I shrugged and shook my head in embarrassment.

"Listen guys," Sal said in a conciliatory tone. "There is no cash. This isn't the fucking stone ages. We've got accounts. Everything's done digitally. Ones and zeros."

"I ain't never seen no electronic money," Virgil said.

"Shut the fuck up, Virgil," I said.

Sal continued, "It's in bank accounts. Bank accounts I don't have access to."

"Well then what the fuck are we supposed to do with you?" I asked.

"Let me go. You haven't hurt me. I've got no reason to fuck with you guys if you just let me go," Sal said.

Virgil picked up the controller next to the door. "Fuck you," he said and flipped the switch.

Nothing happened. I mean, besides Fat Sal screaming like a littler girl while pissed and shat himself.

White Play-Doh is notoriously non-explosive. Though, when shaped into a square and penetrated by wires it can be quite scary. I mean, it worked didn't it? He told me about the money?

"What the fuck?" Virgil said.

I pulled the hunting knife from my jeans pocket and rammed it into Virgil's chest, all the way up to it's deer-antlered hilt. He fell backwards with a thud. In death he wore the same expression as when high, stupid.

"Holy shit," Fat Sal exclaimed from his chair.

"Wal-Mart," I said, pulling the blade from Virgil's heart. "Knives and Play-Doh at every day low prices, always."

"So this is it then? You're gonna kill me? I didn't think you had it in you before..." He nodded at Virgil.

"Virgil was an okay guy. Dumb as all fuck, but okay," I said, inching closer to Sal. "He was a liability, though. And I can't leave any liabilities." Then I sliced his neck like a Christmas ham.

I carried everything --knife, play-doh, wires, bodies-- in trash bags out to the rented pontoon. A sponge was needed to scrub the blood off the floor. Then it, too, went into the boat.

All of it I ferried to the middle of the lake and dumped overboard. The stones I put in the trash bags dragged my troubles away in a few measly seconds.

I returned the pontoon to the marina but the assholes kept my deposit because I'd lost the anchor.

From the Marina I drove to the roadside where I'd first abducted Fat Sal. I got behind the wheel of his Cadillac and turned the key. The engine roared to life and I switched the shifter from P to D and started pulling further off the road. Trees grew thick and I hoped they would hide the vehicle for at least a little while.

Just for giggles, I opened the glove department. Stacks of cash fell into the passenger-side floorboard. Virgil was supposed to have checked the Cadillac's interior while I looked for hiding places on the outside. That stupid asshole.

Dusty Wallace *lives in the Appalachians of Virginia with his wife and two sons. He enjoys reading, writing, and the occasional fine cigar. Find him at DustyVersion.blogspot.com or on Twitter: @CosmicDustMite.*

She Drowns in Dreams

Stephanie Smith

She drowns in dreams,
chlorinated and alone—
these toxic flecks of fairy dust
and gravel forced into blind eyes

I smother her with subliminal thoughts,
recite passages from the Necronomicon
I sing her Faust on better days
when angels plummet to the earth
and our darkest nightmares come out to play

I implore her to embrace the dark
and kiss the worm that feeds on rot

I show her the beauty of ebon night,
the moonlight with its silver tears
She abandons her fear of drowning
and joins me, now, for a midnight swim

Stephanie Smith's *poetry and fiction has appeared in such publications as* Pif Magazine, Strong Verse, The Literary Hatchet, The Horror Zine, *and* Morpheus Tales. *Her first poetry chapbook,* Dreams of Dali, *is available from Flutter Press.*

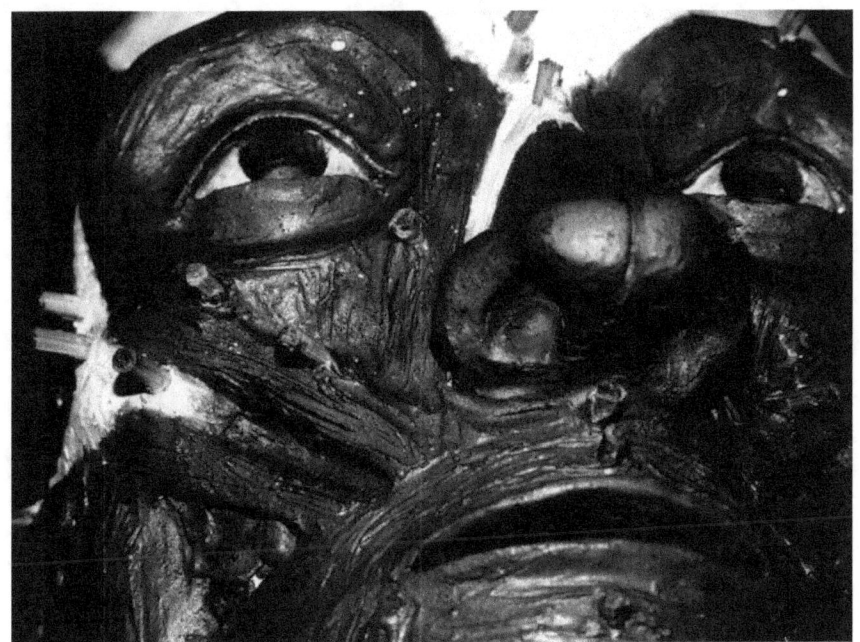

 by Eleanor Leonne Bennett

Eleanor Leonne Bennett *is an internationally award winning photographer andvisual artist. She is the CIWEM Young Environmental Photographer of The Year 2013 and has also won first places with* National Geographic,The World Photography Organisation, Nature's Best Photography *and* The National Trust *to name but a few. Eleanor's photography has been published in the* Telegraph, The Guardian, The British Journal of Psychiatry, Life Force Magazine, British Vogue, Harper's Bazaar *and as the cover of books and magazines extensively throughout the world. Her art is globally exhibited, having shown work in New York, Paris, London, Rome, Los Angeles, Hong Kong, Copenhagen, Washington, Canada, Spain, Japan and Australia amongst many other locations. She was also the only person from the UK to have her work displayed in the National Geographic and Airbus run See The Bigger Picture global exhibition tour with the United Nations International Year Of Biodiversity 2010. In 2012 her work received coverage on ABC Television*

THEY ALWAYS COME IN TWOS

Adam Gaylord

I sneeze.

Immediately their eyes are on me, the rest of the car's passengers looking while pretending not to.

The second sneeze hits me before I can react. I try to stifle it but nature takes its course.

I always sneeze in twos.

The number of visible phones in the car doubles. A woman who had been sitting across the aisle steers her son to the far end of the car with a firm hand. They stand beneath a bright yellow CDC poster, glaring at me over their surgical masks. Under the all too familiar "Stop the Spread" slogan the poster listed the symptoms every still-living American knows by heart.

Sneezing fits.

There's no way two sneezes count as a fit. I always sneeze in twos.

A man three rows up turns and gives me a long look, talking in hushed tones on his cell phone.

I pull the chain, still blocks away from my stop.

Fever.

Of course I'm sweating. It's 100 degrees outside.

The transit slows and I move toward the door, the other passengers stepping quickly aside.

They're waiting for me when the doors open, two men in full air-filtration masks and yellow arm bands.

Nausea.

My stomach churns, from fear I'm sure.

As they lead me away I try to explain, "They always come in twos!"

Adam Gaylord *lives with his beautiful wife, daughter, and less beautiful dog in Loveland, CO. When not at work as a biologist he's usually hiking, drinking craft beer, drawing comics, writing short stories, or some combination thereof. His fantasy novel* Sol of the Coliseum *just came out from Mirror World Publishing. You can check out his stuff at* http://adamsapple2day.blogspot.com/ *or look him up on Goodreads.*

The Music of Angels

Bruce Boston

Here in Heaven,
the music of angels
plays most of the time.

It echoes from the
facades of immaculate
buildings and resonates
on flagstone walkways
and landscaped plazas.

The music of angels
is a celestial music,
a music of spiritual beauty
and spiritual sustenance.

Deft orchestral and
choral arrangements,
golden sheets of sound
all to the glory of God.

Yet there are times
when I must admit
this music begins
to grate on me
more than a little.

There are times
when it begins again
after a few blessed
moments of silence
that I think I may
start to scream.

I need to hear
something different,
something with a beat
that can make
me feel alive.

But this is Heaven.
We are not alive here.

Bruce Boston *is the author of more than fifty books and chapbooks, including the novels* The Guardener's Tale *and* Stained Glass Rain. *His writing has received the Bram Stoker Award, a Pushcart Prize, the Asimov's Readers Award, and the Grand Master Award of the Science Fiction Poetry Association.*

VERMIN

Lisa Lepovetsky

Nobody cleaned a house like Marge Barnswell. Walter and Edie always left little streaks on the windows and hairs or bits of fluff on the furniture. Worst of all, they left tiny crumbs of food on the counters, attracting the attention of the vermin.

"If you don't keep things clean," Marge patiently explained to her husband and daughter, "bugs will notice you. All those little crawling, scurrying things will sniff you right out and creep into your life. And when vermin get in, you can never get rid of them. They're smarter than we are, and they'll gradually take over, without you even realizing. Never draw their attention, never let them know you're here."

She knew more about bugs than she could tell them. Marge grew up on a farm in southeastern Pennsylvania, and had seen what devastation vermin could wreak. Rats, mice, moles, even cute soft rabbits and chipmunks destroyed food and belongings and left their filthy droppings and nasty footprints over everything.

That was bad enough -- but the insects were the worst. They could sneak in anywhere, no matter how well you guarded against them. Some were nearly invisible. And when vermin showed up, they were there forever. They might lose a battle or two, but they always won the war. You might as well give up and move, let them pillage what was left. Marge hated to think what happened to the people who never gave up.

You couldn't let your guard down for even a minute; the vermin were everywhere—waiting, watching. It didn't matter how many times Walter suggested she might be overdoing the sterilization thing when Edie was a baby, or how many well-meaning "friends" raised disapproving eyebrows. Marge wasn't about to let anything happen to *her* daughter. Little girls were the most vulnerable. She must be vigilant.

When Edie was older, Marge often listened at Edie's bedroom door when her daughter had friends over. She had to be sure they didn't have food in the bedroom to draw bugs in from the outside. Marge nodded smugly whenever the other girls talked about cockroach or ant problems in their houses. Her daughter would never complain about those things.

Edie sometimes whined that her school friends rarely visited more than once, and Marge said they weren't real friends, real friends would understand. But the truth was, Marge secretly wished her daughter would stop having friends over to the house altogether. The strain was almost unbearable. She was forced to follow the girls around constantly, picking up after them.

Edie complained to her father when he came home from work, claiming Marge washed out glasses before they were even empty, put away games or clothes before Edie and her friends even had a chance to use them. Walter would listen, shake his head sympathetically, and return to his newspaper with hardly a word.

Once, during the spring of Edie's senior year, Marge had tried to make her daughter understand about the vermin. She'd knocked softly on Edie's door. When Edie answered, Marge shuffled in awkwardly and struggled to find the words that would show Edie why she dreaded people coming into the house.

"You never know what germs or tiny creatures might be carrying with them," she said with a shudder, her hands writhing inside one another like small animals. "Even we have things living on our clothes, in our hair—even" she shuddered again, "inside our bodies. Nobody can get rid of all of them. Some of these bugs are invisible to the naked eye. You can feel them crawling at night on your skin, searching for..." she stopped, her heart beating too fast to continue for a moment.

Edie, her long golden hair haloed by the lamp on her desk, had sighed and looked at her mother in amazement. "Frankly, Mother," she finally said, "I'm amazed I was ever conceived."

Marge had blushed and tried to change the subject, to tell her about the farm, and the awful creepy-crawly things there, but somehow she got mixed up and began thinking about her own long-dead father instead. She tried to tell Edie about how Papa's eyes squinched up real tight when he was angry, and how his huge knuckles were always red and cracked from the harsh weather. But Marge's words got all twisted up and confused, scampering around each other. Edie became impatient.

"Mom, I can't follow what you're saying. Are you saying your father wasn't clean? Is that it?" Marge flinched away from Edie's unexpected insight, but said nothing. "Is that why you're so neurotic about bugs and house-cleaning and stuff?"

Marge just stared at her daughter, so much like herself and yet a complete stranger. She couldn't explain; she didn't know how to say it. Edie was right, but she was wrong. It was more than that, more than just a neurotic reaction to her childhood. Marge knew things about vermin, things she'd learned from years of careful watching when her own mother hadn't been quite able to tell her the truth. Things her father hadn't wanted to know.

Edie's pale eyes begged her mother to tell her something, tell her anything. Marge opened her mouth, not knowing what to say, not even caring what she said.

"It's not that," she began. "I mean, it's not about me. They watch us so they know who's accessible, who's weak, and—"

"*Who* knows?" Edie was frowning, glancing at her clock. "I don't understand you, Mother. You always do this."

Then the phone rang, and the moment was gone.

A month later, the day after graduation, Edie was gone too. She'd found a job in the city, and lived with a friend until she could afford her own place. At first, she came home on weekends and holidays, then just holidays, then a few hours Christmas Eve. Walter didn't seem to mind, but Walter never said much.

Marge felt as though her world had shrunk around her. But she knew that as long as she kept things clean and tidy, she would be safe. And so would Edie. Somehow—Marge wasn't quite sure how—she knew that her constant vigil against the vermin was what had kept Edie from having awful things happen to her. Even though Edie didn't live with them anymore.

Marge never clarified in her own mind just what those 'awful things' were, but it was like having her apartment broken into or losing her job or being murdered in the subway late at night...or worse. What could be worse than being murdered, Marge couldn't imagine—or didn't think she could.

When Walter died, seven years later, Edie spent two days in the Queens house after the funeral, helping her mother pack his things away and take them to the Goodwill. Marge told Edie she was moving uptown to a smaller, more affordable place.

"Your father didn't leave me much of a pension," she said. "And I can't afford the rent on this house anymore. If I'm careful, I can make it on what he left and my social security."

Edie continued packing in silence. Marge knew she was feeling guilty, imagining her mother in a filthy ghetto apartment. She prayed deep down that Edie would suggest the two of them move in together—a least for a while. That way, she could be sure the vermin hadn't found Edie yet. She knew what to look for.

As if reading her mind, Edie looked up. "It wouldn't work, Mom," she said quietly.

"What wouldn't?" Marge asked, startled.

"I'm sorry to have to say this, but I couldn't stand having you live with me."

"Oh. Well I didn't...I mean, I never said that—" Marge babbled awkwardly, fighting the tears that rose in her throat.

"No, but that's what you were thinking." Edie sighed, taping the box closed. "Don't you think I feel like shit? I mean, my own mother. But I've been, well, living with someone for a few months. Our relationship is still in what I'd call the formative stages. I just couldn't bring you in with us now."

"Living with someone? Relationship?" Marge felt the blood leave her limbs, and sat down. She hadn't even known Edie had someone—some man, apparently—in her life. She was letting him touch her and kiss her and.... Marge bit her lip and shuddered, but said nothing.

"I should have said something sooner," Edie said, "but you and I hardly talk anymore. I'll tell you what. I'll do some figuring, and see whether I can come up with enough extra money each month to get you into a nicer place, maybe closer to us. How's that sound?"

And the topic was closed. Edie paid for the moving van to pick up the few things Marge decided to take with her, and left before they got there. To her credit, she called her mother as soon as the phone company hooked up the phone.

"How's the new place?" Edie asked.

"Well, it needs some work," Marge said carefully, looking around her at the dingy walls, the threadbare carpet, the stained fixtures and the gritty coating of filth on everything. "But I'm sure I can manage."

A man's voice said something in the background on Edie's end. Marge ground her teeth as he spoke. His voice was coarse and husky, as though something lived deep in his throat.   "Well, that sounds great," Edie said cheerfully back into the receiver, as though Marge had just told her she'd moved into Versailles. "I can't wait to see it. We'll come for dinner when you're settled." The connection was broken before Marge had a chance to answer.

◌⬧⬥⬧∞

Two days later, Marge sat on the greasy seat of the uptown bus, clutching her shopping bag tighter every time the bus's doors hissed open to allow the hot, rancid wind in. She tucked her skirt under her damp thighs. Not for the first time, Marge wished Edie had invited her to move into her apartment.

Not that Edie's apartment was any Park Avenue condo, not at all. But it was in a respectable neighborhood, where Edie could walk home after dark alone, and where she recognized some of the faces of the people who lived near her. Edie didn't even have cockroaches in her apartment, and that was something few city-dwellers could say. But Marge remembered the gravelly voice on the phone, and knew it was only a matter of time before he contaminated her daughter.

The bus finally reached 104th Street and Marge used one fingertip to touch the electronic strip above her head. The bus driver pulled up to the next curb, and Marge stepped down. Heat bounced off the sidewalk. She walked around the corner, slowly climbing the stoop to the heavy steel door.

The air in the dim hallway was humid. Marge thought she heard some tiny creature scurry into the shadows behind her. She avoided touching the walls as she started up the six steep flights of stairs to her apartment. She tucked her purse into the shopping bag so she could grasp the railing. The narrow piece of old wood felt slimy with fingerprints. It swayed beneath her weight, though she held it as lightly as possible. She reminded herself to call the super about reinforcing it before someone got hurt.

Something scampered lightly along the railing and over her left hand. Marge let go of the railing with a start, and nearly toppled into the dark stairwell. She caught herself, and stumbled up the last flight to her apartment, triple-locking the door behind her. She leaned back on it, breathing heavily. Her heart thudded loudly in her ears.

But when she opened her eyes again, she realized she wasn't home. This apartment wasn't home and never would be. It was just a tiny filthy box tucked among hundreds of other tiny filthy boxes, filled with creatures endlessly scurrying and scampering, producing more of their filthy kind. The grey, greasy walls closed in on Marge, and she saw something scamper behind the refrigerator. A cockroach.

"Oh no, you don't," she said aloud. "Marge Barnswell isn't going to let you win. I won't have you crawling around me, invading my home, my food, my body, leaving dirty little trails I can't wash away. Not again."

Suddenly, Papa's face appeared before her. He had been dead for more than twenty years, killed when his tractor rolled over on him in a ditch. She'd barely thought of him since, other than the uneasy, vague recollection of a nightmare or two. Now here he was, smiling at her from the stained enamel of the refrigerator.

And suddenly, Marge was back in the barn, squeezing herself into the corner of an unused stall, waiting for her father to find her. Hide and seek.

She'd hear him count to one hundred, and then walk away to find her. She cowered, trying to disappear into the pile of straw still left from last winter. Tiny creatures scurried insanely around her, as though they too were trying in vain to escape. In the silence of the summer afternoon, there seemed to be so many of them, they could take over the world. Mice and rats squeaked angrily at one another, fighting over a hideout or some morsel of food. Flies and gnats whined around her head, and something with too many legs crawled down the back of her shirt. Little Margie gasped and shuddered, but dared not move until her father found her.

What if this time he never came, just forgot about her?

She'd finally decide to give up and call out to him. And when she opened her mouth, the vermin came in. They'd been waiting, too, and as she drew in a deep lungful of the stale, decaying air deep beneath the straw, she felt things enter her—unclean things that flew and crawled and jumped eagerly into her. She wanted to scream, but couldn't. But no matter how long it seemed she waited, he always came, always remembered.

Back in her urban kitchen, Marge Barnswell whined softly as the memory bored into her brain. She shook her head and pushed her hands hard against her eyes to dispel the memory, then reached into her shopping bag. She pulled out a huge spray can, with the black, stylized picture of a giant cockroach on the label. Marge pulled the cap off and dropped it with a clatter onto the linoleum. She leaned forward as though she were stalking the refrigerator.

"I'm going to get every last one of you," Marge muttered. "I'm ready for you now, you hateful bastards." She'd never used that word before, always claiming, as Papa had, that dirty words made for dirty lives. But it felt delicious on her tongue now.

She said it again, louder. "You bastards."

First, Marge sprayed can after can of insect killer in every corner of her apartment, around every baseboard, behind each appliance and fixture, and into every crevice and crack, no matter how tiny. The smell made her gag at first, but she told herself it was killing the bad things, and after a while she got used to it. Maybe it would kill the tiny bugs that lived in her body, making her dirty where she couldn't reach with the soap and cleansers.

Then she pulled out rodent poison, sprinkling it like holy water around the edges of her moldy carpet and in dark lines along the edges of each tiny room, including the closet. She liked to imagine the furry little monsters choking and dying alone in the darkness of their hideouts.

The phone rang, and Marge considered not answering it. There was only one person who might call, and Marge didn't know whether she felt up to a conversation with Edie tonight. Finally, unable to deny her daughter, she picked it up on the eighth ring, wiping the mouthpiece with her sleeve.

"Mom?" Edie sounded concerned. "I've been calling all afternoon. Where were you?"

"Why?"

"What do you mean, why?"

Marge was impatient to get back to work. She wanted to finish her work before the vermin discovered what she was up to and became angry before she finished. "Why did you call, Edie?"

"Oh. Well, Steve and I have something to talk to you about. We thought we might come over tonight. Is that okay?"

"No," Marge said quickly. She couldn't remember the last time she'd denied her daughter something important.

"Mom? What did you say?"

"I said no. Not tonight. I'm very busy tonight."

"Busy?" Edie was silent for a minute. "Mother, are you all right?" She spoke very carefully.

"I'm fine," Marge answered, disturbed by the long interruption. She thought she heard something moving in the ceiling.

"What are you doing?"

"I'm cleaning. Getting rid of bugs and things, actually. This place is a mess, completely infested. All these old buildings are."

"Well, can't you take a break later? This is really important. Steve and I—-"

"Look, Edie," Marge cut her off, "I really can't. I've been spraying and laying out poison, but I still have to caulk."

"Caulk?"

"Yes. That's my new idea." Marge paused to catch her breath. "I'm going to caulk and plaster every crack and crevice in the place, until there's nowhere for the little bastards to get in. But I have to do it quickly, before they realize what I'm up to."

Marge barely heard Edie's tiny gasp, because she was holding her free ear against the wall. She was sure she heard something moving in there.

"Mom, I think Steve and I better come over."

"No. I told you, not tonight. Maybe tomorrow." Marge suddenly had a terrible thought. "Edie, what do you suppose they'll do?"

"Who, Mom?"

"The vermin—the roaches and spiders and things. Do you think they'll figure out how to get in the door? Are they that smart?"

"I don't think so, Mom. Listen, why don't you—"

Again, Marge cut her off. "I'll call you tomorrow, Edie. Everything will be fine then." She hung up. A moment later, she took the receiver off the hook, so she wouldn't be bothered again.

The first thing Marge caulked was the front door. She wasn't about to be ambushed. "You think you're so smart," she muttered, as she smeared the slimy white gunk thickly into the spaces around the door. "You have to get up pretty early in the morning to fool Margie Barnswell. You better watch your step."

She ran her fingers around the door several times, spreading the clean white ooze of caulking, then did the same with the grimy window that opened onto the fire escape. Around and around the window, then on to the bathroom and kitchen fixtures, forcing the last of the rubbery goo into the crevices, leaving bits of her fingernails in it like tiny red mites. Marge's breath whistled through her teeth, and her shoulders began cramping, but she had to keep going. She had to finish sealing her apartment before they caught on. This was her last chance.

"I'll show you," she mumbled over and over, as she mixed up the spackling compound. "I'll show you this time.

Finally, hours later—days later, it seemed to Marge—she was finished. She surveyed her handiwork. Thick white smears of caulking and spackling compound encircled the doors and window, and stretched, crisscrossing, across the walls like snail trails. She had even pulled up the ancient carpet and smeared caulking between the floorboards and along the baseboards of the rooms. Piled in the center of the living room were empty cans of insect killer and caulking tubes.

"You'll never get in now," Marge said, raising one tired fist. "I'm an impenetrable fortress, pure and unsoiled. Margie Barnswell wins again."

Then she heard it. Tiny scurrying sounds in the walls, in the ceiling. Faint at first, the sound grew quickly, until it seemed as though the very air around her were alive with tiny scampering feet and chitinous wings and vibrating antennae. Marge jammed her fists over her ears, but the sounds were as loud as ever—louder, even. The vermin were everywhere, and they were determined to find a way in.

"No, you can't get in," she screamed. "I won't let you in."

When she glanced at the door, she screamed again. The door to her apartment was shuddering and vibrating beneath the pressure of millions of crawling, scritching little feet and claws. She hadn't imagined they would—could—find the forces to actually break down a solid door. There couldn't be that many of them. The chain on her lock rattled as the pulsing pressure began forcing the old heavy door in, tearing the molding away from the walls. The caulking loosened with a nasty sucking noise.

When the door finally tore open with a violent splintering, Marge screamed and ran into the living room to cower in a far corner. A tall wave of vermin headed straight for her. Every cockroach, fly, spider, ant, and beetle in the city seemed to have found its way to Marge's apartment door. Thousands, millions of crawling, scampering, clicking, buzzing, squeaking creatures piling one on another, climbing over each other in an ever-shifting shape, their legs and glossy wings in perpetual motion.

Suddenly, the wave picked itself up as it reached the woman curled in the far corner. The forward legions backed up into the rear battalions, piling up higher and higher, until the mass of swarming insects stood more than five feet high, towering over Marge. She looked up to see a crawling, distorted parody of her father's face. She wept.

"Daddy?" she tried to ask, but her heart beat too fast in her chest, and she could only gasp. She closed her eyes and curled into a ball, waiting.

When a hand touched her arm, Marge jumped back, hitting her head against the wall behind her. When she opened her eyes, Edie was leaning over her.

"Mom? Are you okay?"

Marge's eyes darted around the apartment. Where were the vermin? "They're hiding," she croaked. "They're waiting to get me."

"Who, Mom? Who's going to get you? There's nobody here."

Then Marge understood. It wasn't her the vermin wanted—it was Edie. This had all been a ruse to get Edie to come over so they could crawl all over her, get inside her, contaminate her with their filth. Marge dragged herself off the floor and grabbed her daughter's arms.

"You have to get out of here," she hissed into her daughter's startled face. "It's you they're after."

As Marge pushed her daughter backward toward the open door, she heard them again. A wave of scampering, fluttering and buzzing began in the wall behind her, and moved through the walls and ceiling toward them like electricity. Marge had to protect Edie, had to save her. As they reached the doorway, she heard the vermin all around her and pushed harder.

Edie's heel caught on one of the loose boards from the broken doorframe, and she stumbled backward out the doorway. Marge still clutched desperately to her daughter, and they fell against the railing. The old wood gave way beneath their combined weight and splintered. They fell six stories into darkness.

When the first-floor residents peered from their doorways to see what caused the screams, they saw Edie's broken body on the cement floor, a thin stream of blood oozing from beneath her skull. Marge's body lay on top of her daughter's, arms spread to the sides in a protective gesture.

Nobody noticed the large cockroach that scurried from under them to disappear beneath one of the closed doors.

Lisa Lepovetsky *earned her MFA in creative writing from Penn State, and has published dozens of poems and stories in magazines and anthologies, such as:* EQMM, Dark Destiny, Blood Muse, Cemetery Dance, 100 Vicious Little Vampire Stories, *and many others.*

The Patron Saint of Rubberneckers

Noel Sloboda

You promise yourself: never
again succumb to the tyrannical
spell of mere curiosity.

And so you forget
about him, secreted
behind the driver's seat

for weeks on end, silent
and still while you roll
back and forth from work

crisscrossing byways—
until shards of glass
spill across hot blacktop

and catch flashes of blue;
or an upside-down tanker leaks
gallons of goo that smells

like moldering meat;
or a splash of crimson
stains the grill of a car

the same make and model as yours.
Tender but unspeaking,
he splays a warm palm

atop your skull
and as your spine jellies,
your head swivels

turning and turning till it feels
as if your neck must
snap. Then you speed up

again, free to pretend
you are alone, refocus
on broken lines and

fume about lost time.

Noel Sloboda's *work has lately been in* Harpur Palate, Nimrod, The Midwest Quarterly, *and* Weave. *He is the author of the poetry collections* Shell Games *(sunnyoutside, 2008) and* Our Rarer Monsters *(sunnyoutside, 2013) as well as several chapbooks.*

Retribution, or, The nest-Collector's fate

J. J. Steinfeld

Cletus went from passionate birding into obsessive nest-collecting, despite warnings from other birders that what he was doing was reprehensible if not illegal. He argued that he never took nests with birds actually in them or anywhere nearby, often describing his fascination with the beauty and efficacy of bird's nests as divinely-inspired.

On his fiftieth birthday, with no one else around to criticize him, Cletus climbed a tree in his favourite woods, a ten-minute drive from his home, and found a nest with a huge egg, about half the size of his own rather large head. The egg was a blood-red colour. This rare find excited Cletus, and as he was climbing down the tree, he fell, but was only slightly bruised, and miraculously, the nest and egg were undamaged, what he took as a divine sign that he was allowed to keep his amazing find and continue with his nest-collecting. Didn't the Bible say that man had dominion over all creatures in existence, in the sea, on earth, and fowl of the air were specifically mentioned, *Genesis* 1:26, he knew his Bible.

Cletus took this magnificent nest and huge egg to his basement, where he kept his vast collection of nests, a collection that he wanted to increase and fill his entire house with one day. After placing the new nest and egg atop a cardboard carton close to the stairs, he counted his nests, and to his delight this was the two hundredth, feeling an elation from the number and glorious collection. In his mind, he set a goal of a thousand nests, but had no idea how long it would take him to gather that monumental number.

Eventually the huge blood-red egg hatched into an oversized bird, strange in appearance but lovely all the same, which he kept as a pet and gave the run of his house, apart from his own small bedroom. At first he thought it might be a buzzard or a vulture, not that he knew the difference, yet when he checked his bird-watcher's guides, of which he had many, he could not find a bird exactly like his usual find.

On his fifty-first birthday, after returning home with another bird's-nest, the two-hundred and fiftieth, Cletus heard frightening noises from his bedroom. Inside, the room was destroyed, feathers every-where, the window broken, no bird in sight. All the pages from all of his bird-watcher's guides had been ripped out and scattered around the room. Cletus looked for his cherished Bible, as if to find solace or a passage that might explain this destruction, but the Bible was missing.

Canadian fiction writer, poet, and playwright J. J. Steinfeld *lives on Prince Edward Island, where he is patiently waiting for Godot's arrival and a phone call from Kafka. While waiting, he has published sixteen books, including* Disturbing Identities *(Stories, Ekstasis Editions),* Should the Word Hell Be Capitalized? *(Stories, Gaspereau Press),* Would You Hide Me? *(Stories, Gaspereau Press),* An Affection for Precipices *(Poetry, Serengeti Press),* Misshapenness *(Poetry, Ekstasis Editions),* Word Burials *(Novel and Stories, Crossing Chaos Enigmatic Ink),* A Glass Shard and Memory *(Stories, Recliner Books),* Identity Dreams and Memory Sounds *(Poetry, Ekstasis Editions), and* Madhouses in Heaven, Castles in Hell *(Stories, Ekstasis Editions). More than three-hundred of his short stories and seven-hundred poems have appeared in anthologies and periodicals internationally, and over forty of his one-act plays and a handful of full-length plays have been performed in Canada and the United States.*

Radiant Night

Bob Johnston

As I wended my way through the dreary wasteland, buffeted by the awesome forces of an unrelenting gale and horizontal sheets of rain, the ground was illumined by a continuous, dazzling display of heavenly fireworks, silent lightning on a scale I had never before witnessed.

In my path, every rock protruding above the foul sea of mud emitted its own ghastly green glow, evoking old, obscene memories of mold and vomit. Their macabre radiance served as guideposts keeping me on the path. I stopped to rest, and the lightning ceased immediately. The driving rain continued to attack me in eerie silence. Blinded and choked by the rain beating into my eyes and nostrils, I could barely discern a distant light, a flickering pinpoint of blue. The same light had appeared to me a half-hour earlier, and now it seemed no closer, receding as I advanced.

Little rested, I resumed my struggle along the path; and as if on cue, the silent aerial display began again. Each of my steps was accompanied by a horrible sucking sound as I pulled free of the mud. The torrential rain continued, the mud became deeper, and the foul smell intensified, now resembling that of a perfumed, rotting corpse. Exhausted after only a few minutes, I sank to my knees. Again, the lightning ceased immediately.

    As the mud rose up to claim me, I struggled to my feet, only to accelerate my descent into the lower depths. Now the mud itself glowed, an unholy green. As it closed my nostrils, I knew the final truth: I will be preserved eternally, the last specimen of *Homo anything*.

Bob Johnston *is a retired petroleum engineer, translator of Russian literature, and an ex-drunk. He started to write serious poetry at age sixty; and now, more than three decades later, he is still trying to catch up. His poems have appeared in twenty-odd journals and in a collection of his poetry titled* At the Rim *(Sunstone Press, 2011). His poems reflect a dim view of the universe and outrage at having been propelled into a century he will never understand.*

1:23

Kyle Owens

A man with headphones gazes through glass.

"Three, two, one..."

"Welcome back. It's 1:23 AM and I'm Bob Carson and you're listening to City after Dark. Let's get back to the phones. Hello? What's on your mind tonight?"

Falls of silence filters strong.

"You're on the air caller. Go right ahead."

Bob notices the rolling eyes of his producer before his earphones draw in a voice.

"Who am I talking to?" asks the caller.

"Everybody."

Listeners senses arouse forward in the quiet linger of darkness.

"Are you still there caller?"

No stirs of sound voices the night.

"Caller?"

"I'm here."

The male voice was deep. Shadowy. It seems to be just outside the grasp of reality's stare.

"Great. What's your name?"

The caller's mind stumbles for a response.

"I-my-I don't want to say."

"Fair enough. I was just talking about the Monday night football game before we came back on the air. Did you see it?"

"I don't watch football."

"What do you watch?"

"The news. I always watch the news and read the newspapers."

"Did you want to talk about something you saw on the news?"

"Yeah. Well, I don't—"

Bob waits for the caller to continue, but only stray shadows fills his headphones.

"Are you still there caller?"

"Yeah."

"Tell me what's on your mind?"

"I'm—I'm just fed up with the world."

"We all have days like that. Where it seems like everything goes wrong. It gives you a feeling of frustration and hopelessness. Is that how you're feeling now?"

Boldness soldier's forward.

"I don't feel hopeless anymore."

"How so?"

"It's best to try and take the initiative. Instead of adapting you should try to stop things."

"Stop what things?"

"Things I don't like."

"What don't you like?"

The conversation turns to its edge.

"Listen to me. I've put a bomb in the city and if you don't convince me to not activate it, then I'm killing people tonight. You've got ten minutes."

Bob's eyes flashes through the glass into the face of fear of his producer on the other side. The producer mouths the words, "I'll call the police" and begins to place the call.

"You now have nine minutes," the voice of violence says in a quiet tone.

Bob's mind races for speech, words, sentences, thoughts, but nothing crests his lips.

"I-I don't-why? Why are you doing this? How does killing someone make things better?"

"It removes the helplessness."

"But you're putting the helplessness on the family of the person you kill. You know how the feeling of helplessness makes you feel. Why would you put this same feeling on someone else?"

"To regain control of your life you have to control that of another."

"You can't just kill someone for no reason."

"I have my reasons!" the caller screams out.

Thoughts boil. Control spirals.

"Let's calm down now."

"You have eight minutes!"

"Hear me out. We don't need to go around setting off bombs or anything. There's other ways to deal with the emotions you're feeling. Remember, the person you kill isn't the only person effected by the act. They have family and friends. They may be someone important to society possibly not now but maybe in the future or they may bring someone into the world or inspire someone that has an impact on the society for the good. And you can't rule out that the impact they have could be to you in a very positive way."

The wait for a response silhouettes midnight.

"You have seven minutes."

Bob looks into the producer's booth and he holds up a piece of paper that reads, "Stall. Police on the way."

"You said you had your reasons for this. What are they?"

"The world thinks all of my beliefs are wrong and I'm tired of it. When I try to explain to them what I'm feeling and believe they shut me down. They don't even have the decency to listen to my argument. I will not be bullied out of my beliefs anymore. I'll do the bullying now."

"What are your beliefs? I'm interested in knowing what you think."

Blunts of silence slowly creeps into sound.

"Your insincerity angers me."

"I mean it. I want to know your beliefs. This is why I do this job. To learn about the people in this city."

"You're just trying to keep me on the line until the police arrive. That doesn't sound like you're interested in my thoughts to me."

"You can't just kill innocent people. That's not going to get you any sympathy for your beliefs."

"They aren't innocent people. I'm not just randomly doing this. I've thought it through. I've picked my targets. You have five minutes."

Fear slits Bob's face. Words tangle raw inside his mind. Smears of actions round smooth.

"You have four minutes."

"Look. You can't do this. It's too devastating not only to the people directly involved, but to the city as a whole. We're all in this together in this thing called life. I know there are some bad people in the world. People that aren't giving you any respect. But we can't lose our morality in a revenge mentality that it doesn't matter anymore. Life is too precious for that."

A draw of nothingness answers his pleas.

"Are you there caller?"

Red needles set motionless on the control boards resting for voices.

"Caller, are you there?"

The producer looks at Bob with sharp grey eyes and shakes his head no.

Bob looks at the clock and he has two minutes left on the imposed deadline.

"Ladies and gentlemen, I don't know if this was real or some sort of prank or what."

In the producer's booth, a police officer walks in. Bob immediately gets up to talk to the officer, but then informs the audience, "I'm going to play some music here now folks. See if I can regroup."

Bob hit some buttons on the radio board and then takes off his headset. The producer motions for Bob to come into the booth to which Bob heads inside.

The officer greets Bob with a handshake.

"I'm Officer Wilson. I was listening in on the way over."

Bob was still shaking.

"I've never had anything like this happen before. Do you think it was a sick prank or was this real?"

"No, I'm real," the officer said.

The officer tears open his shirt exposing a bomb. He looks at Bob, smiles, then pushes the button in his right hand.

Kyle Owens *lives in the Appalachian Mountains and his work has appeared in* Aberrant Literature, Jimson Weed, *several anthologies and his mockumentary screenplay,* Fairfield Music Festival *is in pre-production with Claude Reid Productions.*

THE THIRST OF THE WAVES *by Denny E. Marshall*

Denny E Marshall *has had art, poetry and fiction published, some recently.*
To see more of his works visit his website at www.dennymarshall.com

A VILLANELLE FOR A VILLIAN

Deborah Guzzi

Was I not too young, tell me truly, speak?
The dew of life was still upon my face;
when I refused to take that final leap

to loose my life when not yet at its peak.
I took a deathly kiss in his embrace.
Was I not too young, tell me truly, speak?

Unwise, unwise was I, or simply meek.
How I mortally erred was a disgrace,
when I refused to take that final leap.

No life was this, no haven for the weak,
eternal, soulless, hell no resting place.
Was I not too young, tell me truly, speak?

Existence now bares a fetid reek;
I've replaced the grace of heaven chaste,
when I refused to take that final leap.

I face the nightmares now, hear the shrieks.
Ah, remember there was dew on my face.
Was I not too young, tell me truly, speak?
When I refused to take that final leap.

Deborah Guzzi *is a healing facilitator specializing in Shiatsu and Reiki. She writes for Massage and Aromatherapy Magazines. She travels to expand her knowledge of healing and to seek writing inspiration. She has walked the Great Wall of China, seen Nepal (during the civil war), Japan, Egypt (two weeks before 'The Arab Spring'), Peru, and France during December's terrorist attacks. Her poetry appears in:* Existere - Journal of Arts and Literature *in* Canada, Tincture *in* Australia, Cha:Asian Literary Review, *China,* Latchkey Tales *in* New Zealand, Vine Leaves Literary Journal *in* Greece, *and* Bete Noir, Liquid Imagination, Illumen, Sweet Dreams and Night Terrors, Dead Snakes, Literary Hatchet, Silver Blade *and others in the USA.*

THANATOPIA

Jason Lairamore

Warden Billings stood in the execution chamber wearing the three piece suit he always wore for such occasions. If all went as planned, inmate Helen Barger would die in a few minutes.

"Are you sure that thing will kill her?" he asked the pretty, young woman beside him. She was Dr. Whitney Carson, the inventor of a new virtual reality cybernetic system. Today they were testing one of her programs called the Thanatopia procedure.

"Yes," the doctor answered as she opened the metal case she'd broughtg. The apparatus inside looked like a grease gun with a needle on one end and a bundle of wires coming from the other.

"It's just ... Helen Barger was the head of a brutal drug gang. She's killed dozens of people. There will be a lot of folks on site to watch her die."

Dr. Carson stopped what she was doing and looked around at the plain gray tiles that covered the execution room from floor, wall, and ceiling.

"My virtual reality is the future," she said. "The possibilities of what it might do are endless."

"Like kill somebody," the Warden added.

She nodded. "The government won't fund more research until after human studies. They chose death, not me."

"And you're *sure* this doesn't violate the 8th amendment?" The Warden asked.

Dr. Carson sighed. "Stop worrying. I have a copy of Congress approval, same as you. The procedure will cause internal effects comparable to death by lethal injection."

The Warden checked his watch. Helen Barger should be on her way.

"Why do you call it Thanatopia?"

"'Thanatos', means death and 'Topia', means place. I've created a place to die."

"Sounds like you created Hell."

A pair of guards arrived with Helen Barger strapped to a gurney. As soon as they pushed her into the room, her eyes went to the glass where, soon, people would watch her die.

"Hello Helen, do you remember me?" Dr. Carson asked.

"You're the shrink who asked all the questions," Helen answered.

"That's right." She began applying adhesive pads to Helen's head and chest. "These pads will measure your physiological responses."

"You need all that just to kill me?"

Dr. Carson nodded. "Those questions I asked were to find out your worst fear. When that needle," she pointed to the device from the case, "goes into your spinal column, the answer to that question will come and kill you."

Helen frowned up at her. "I'm going to get eaten by a fucking shark?"

"That is the specified reality I programmed into the device, yes."

Helen remained quiet from then on. The room behind the glass filled with people. The Warden stood off to the side, against the wall, and waited for the clock to strike 3:00.

Helen's head and shoulders had been elevated and a portion of the gurney removed so that Dr. Carson could insert the needle in the proper place.

3:00 arrived.

"Helen Barger, have you any final words?" the Warden asked.

Helen eyed the crowd before speaking. "I'm not done," she said slowly.

The wall behind the warden disintegrated and he disappeared in a cloud of debris. Dr. Carson was tossed back, taken off the floor, to crash against one of the machines. She was too consumed with trying to breathe to even know if she was hurt. She heard snatches of screams and occasional gunshots. Over it all, she heard Helen Barger's manic laughter.

As if by some trick, Helen was suddenly standing above her, bleeding from a dozen different places. In her hand, she held the Thanatopia device.

"And they call me a monster," she said.

A man came to stand beside her. "Helen, let's go. Move your ass." He ran off.

Helen nodded in the direction the man had gone. "There's one of my friends. Where are your friends?"

Dr. Carson tried to move. Everything hurt.

Helen shook her head then eyed the needle in her hand.

"I'm not really scared of sharks," she said. "I'm not scared of anything."

She bent down until her face was inches from Dr. Carson's.

"I tell you what." She wrenched the doctor's head down. "Why don't you try that fucking shark out?" She stabbed the thick point of the needle deep into the doctor's neck.

Dr. Carson screamed as everything went dark.

The water was cold and murky. Anything could be hidden in those depths, but Dr. Carson already knew. She'd designed this reality. She screamed and thrashed. It all felt so real. Something bumped her leg and frantic energy jerked through her limbs in a shockwave. She scanned the dark horizon. She was all alone, as she knew she would be, alone in a place of death.

A slashing pain made her gasp, but she was already being pulled under. Salty water went down her throat as she flailed uselessly against what was to come.

Jason Lairamore *is a writer of science fiction, fantasy, and horror who lives in Oklahoma with his beautiful wife and their three monstrously marvelous children. His work is both featured and forthcoming in over 40 publications to include* Sci Phi Journal, Perihelion Science Fiction, Stupefying Stories *and* Third Flatiron *publications to name a few.*

www.ingramcontent.com/pod-product-compliance
Lightning Source LLC
Chambersburg PA
CBHW071224130626
46555CB00004B/1839